CW00853907

<u>Chapter one</u>

I wake to the sound of the shouting up the stairs.

'Noah, you're going to be late!'

It's September sixth, and not only is it my first day of school, it's the first day back with my friends, and some of them can be real idiots sometimes.

So I guess you could say I'm not looking forward to it, I'm going into year eleven, the final year of being in the same surroundings day in, and day out.

Although my friend group is mostly loud, most of the time annoying guys there are a couple I couldn't see my life without for example Jacob, me and Jacob have been friends for as long as I can remember, he's always been a really great friend to me, we don't hang out like we used to, but we are still always there for each other when needed.

Then you have Gabriel, he is loud, very very loud! The one who thinks every single girl in the school fancies him, when that probably isn't the case, in fact i know that's not the case because if it was he would have a girlfriend by now, but he is still very much single.

Then there is Max. He is like Gabriel's shadow. They are always together. He is also loud, although not as loud as Gabriel.

Max has a girlfriend named Maddie. She is a quiet girl, but she seems nice enough. They got together last year because Gabriel set them up and they have been together ever since.

We have a few girls that occasionally hang around with us at school, people say it's just because they want to be in with 'the popular guys' however I don't even slightly consider myself 'a popular boy' but I'm sure Gabriel and Max would say otherwise.

They like to sit on the field, speaking about the girls and wolf whistling at the ones they think are 'hot'

. I have never really been into joining in with that. I just kind of sit and watch, then being loud and annoying doesn't end at school. It's all the time and honestly it can be quite bloody embarrassing at times.

For example, before we broke up for half-term, we were all sitting on the field like we do every single day, and have done for the last four years, Gabriel thought he would take it upon himself to set me up with one of our friends, Jazmine.

I think it went even as far as a date, if you can call it that, it was just us both sitting in KFC, eating and sitting in silence, the only words we actually spoke was 'hi' and 'bye' when meeting and leaving.

And of course Gabriel wasn't happy about this situation when he found out it didn't go how he wanted it too, and he made it very clear that i should have been grateful he set this date up with Jazmine, he must have asked over one hundred times why i didn't make a move to kiss her.

He can be a right idiot sometimes, he thinks if he keeps pushing, and pushing then people will do exactly what he wants them too, maybe that is the case, and i have to admit i have done in the past with things that aren't relationship related.

This time i think i need to do what i want, and that is to not date Jazmine, of course she's a beautiful girl.

Sometimes I think something must be wrong with me, especially when I have all my friends liking lots of different girls. Well, most of them I have one friend, Ellis, he is bisexual, and he is not afraid of anybody knowing. I find that so admirable.

I have even on occasion debated if i don't like girls at all, like maybe im gay, or bisexual, but i don't find myself attracted to guys either, at least not yet.

Mum and dad say that it will come, and when I meet the right girl I will know, and I should just be happy, young and enjoy my life without worrying about who, or what I am right now, so that's what I've been doing, much to Gabriels dismay.

He likes to tell every single person who he comes into contact with that he is the reason Max has a girlfriend and that is true, but is there a need for everyone else to know?

He set Max and Maddie up a bit like he did with me and Jazmine, except his matchmaking skills did not do too well that time, and he likes to think he's some kind of cupid, so that hurt his feelings.

The first lesson of the new term went as I expected, Gabriel telling the whole class about the 'Amazing' summer holiday he has had, while everybody sits in awe of his words.

My summer holiday was pretty boring, except for a few trips out with my friends, it's been pretty much sitting in my room, playing video games, visiting my nan and grandad, and helping mum and dad renovate the garden, i don't think many people would call that a very exciting six weeks, especially for a sixteen-year-old.

I've always been kind of chilled out. I'm not one who wants to stand out, although other people wouldn't believe that when they meet my friend's group.

In all honesty I like to think I'm nothing like them, at least I try not to be, I would much rather just sit and play on my Xbox, watch movies, and lay in bed, where they would rather be at the next big party.

The next lesson is maths. It's one of the lessons I find the hardest, like don't get me wrong, I know adding and subtracting but algebra? Who needs to learn that? And when is it ever even used?

Walking in to the classroom,

'Welcome back, year eleven,' Mr Radwell shouts across the classroom.

Everybody loves Mr Radwell, he's a pretty cool teacher to be honest, but he does tend to shout a lot which is quite annoying, the class is pretty much the same people from last term, except a couple of new people, and a one person who was in the class above last term, i don't i really know her though, she is very quiet, and spends most breaks and lunches in the library. Gabriel would say she's a 'nerd' but I think she is just staying out of his way, actually all of our way because hanging around with Gabriel automatically gets you the 'loud and nasty' boy title, and who would want that for themselves? Me, apparently.

They are my friends though, and really the only friends i have ever known, and although Gabriel can be the most annoying person you have ever met, he would also stick up for you in any situation, and that is good to have.

The next few lessons go by really quickly and before I know it the first day back is almost over.

'Who wants to come to mine after school?' Max asks as we are all walking to our last lesson of the day.

Of course everybody said yes, they all love to sit around after school, drinking pepsi, eating crisps, and talking about the hottest girls in the school.
I just kind of exist in these conversations, and nod and agree once in a while when I think I should.

'Did you see that new boy today, the one with the curly hair?' Max asks, laughing.

The rest of the guys laugh along, I'm not sure what is funny, but I kind of force out a laugh to make it look like I actually understand what the hell they are talking about, when in reality i didn't even pay enough attention to the new kids in the class, I knew they were there, but that's about it.

'I bet he's gay,' Gabriel say's thought fits of laughter
'He does look pretty gay to me' Max add's laughing so hard now he can barely breath.

I'm not sure what is funny, or why they are laughing so hard at something that isn't even funny, i think by now I'm just laughing because they sound like absolute idiots, but of course they think I'm laughing at them mocking somebody they don't even know, they seem to be good at that it makes their ego a little bigger I guess.
The next day, arriving at school fashionably late as usual, i have a real hard time getting up early so when the alarm goes i snooze it about six times before i actually think, 'crap i need to get up' when i do finally get up, i'm rushing around to leave the house in approximately ten minutes, but somehow i'm still always late.
I walk into the classroom knowing full well I'm about to get detention for being late once again. I think the last term of school I think I must have had three detentions a week, all for being late to class.

'You're late again Noah' Mr Radwell shouts at me across the classroom as i enter,

I say sorry, but i don't actually mean it, and i will most likely be later again tomorrow morning, sitting down in my seat i remember the conversation from the night before with Gabriel and Max, them speaking about the 'new boy' who 'must be gay' because he looks it, whatever that means.
I look around the classroom and spot who they were speaking about, i wouldn't say he 'looks gay' but then again, I don't think anybody looks it, anybody can be any sexuality and look however they want to look, and dress however they want too, without awful people commenting on that.

Seeing me look over, Gabriel nods as if to say 'see i told ya' but in all honesty i don't anything other than a guy, being himself whether that be gay, bisexual, straight or any other Sexuality. He may or may not be, yes he is wearing black nail varnish but guys can wear nail varnish, plus it is against school rules, i guess that makes him pretty cool.

Sitting on the field at lunchtime, Gabriel is doing his usual shouting out to every girl that walks within one foot of him. They normally tell him to piss off and he just laughs it off.

I sometimes think I should do something else, maybe try and make some new friends but then I don't like the thought of having to explain why I want other friends, so I very quickly change my mind.

A few months into the new school term and Gabriel is still being the biggest idiot to everybody, most of the time me included, I think he thinks it's a joke sometimes, but sometimes it doesn't feel like he's joking.

He can either make you feel super safe, and like he would stand up for you at any time, then make you feel like you're worthless and I think the main reason he does it to me is because I don't want to date any of the girls he chooses for me.

Thinking about it lately, I should probably get a girlfriend just to shut him up, so when a few weeks later he's setting me up on yet another date, this time with a girl named Narla.

I agree, of course, and Gabriel is super happy with himself and can't help but tell everybody he knows that he made it happen. I don't know why he is so proud when he makes these things happen.

The days leading up to the date and I start to wish I hadn't agreed when all I've heard is Gabriel and Max asking almost daily where I'm taking her, or what I'm wearing, I don't even know myself.

Before I know it, it's Saturday and the day of my much dreaded date. I haven't even decided what we are going to do, but I'm thinking of something that doesn't involve much talking, maybe cinema? But then she might expect me to be all cuddly and want me to hold her hand, and the thought makes me cringe.

I've never really thought about my sexuality much. It's just something I've never really had to think about. I'm not ready for any kind of relationship with anyone, but having friends like Gabriel and Max, I'm expected to be your typical straight boy.

Back at school on Monday, Gabriel was the first person to ask all the questions.

Did I kiss her? Am I going to see her again? The truth is I did kiss her. I guess I was hoping to feel the spark all of my friends speak about, but I felt nothing, only regret, regret that I was leading her on, and regret that I was letting my friends down.

The truth is i did kiss her, but that was only because she made the first move and i didn't want to make things weird for her,

'Yeah, we kissed' I say quietly,

Gabriel throws his arm around me, squeezing a little tighter every time he says another word.

'Noah kissed Narla, he finally has a girlfriend' he shouts across the field, i don't think i have ever been so embarrassed in my whole life, and before i know it Narla and her friends are

walking towards us, this is like my worst nightmare and i just know Gabriel and Max are going to have a great time making me feel like a right idiot.
Narla walks straight up to me, grabbing hold of my hands while I just stand unsure what to do next.

'Aww look, Noah has his first girlfriend! How cute!'

I can feel myself getting more and more embarrassed by the minute Gabriel is loving it. He knows how awkward I am, and he's taking full advantage of it.
Anyway, I never agreed to be anybody's boyfriend so technically I do not have my first girlfriend, but it doesn't look like that right now, as Narla is standing in front of me, holding on to my hands, kissing me on the cheek, and at one point even smacking my bum.
I'm so glad when it's time to go back to lesson i want to never speak or see Narla again, but that is hard when Gabriel already took it upon himself to arrange out second date, he says he is 'just doing me a favour' but i think really, he's scared to date any of these girls himself so he just sets everybody else up with them instead.
By now it's six months later and I'm still dating Narla. I have tried to break it off many times but Gabriel always makes sure that it doesn't happen.
When I meet with Narla, we spend most of our time at the cinema, if not at her house, watching a movie. I've grown to like her but I think of her as a friend and nothing more than that.
I think the most embarrassing thing about all of this is every time we are around anyone that does not know about me and Narla, Gabriel takes it upon himself to let everybody know that i spent the weekend at Narlas when technically it was only a couple of hours, but of course everybody thinks i spend the whole weekend there, and you can guess what they think we do, but that definitely does not happen.

'Everybody listen, the residential trip is in two weeks. Make sure you bring everything you need' Mr Radwell shouts across the classroom,
I haven't been looking forward to this trip I think mainly because I don't know who I'm going to be spending a week sharing a small dorm with, and it's a sports trip, so I will literally be sleeping, eating, and playing different sports, which doesn't sound very fun to me.

The morning of the trip, everybody is posting on Instagram about how excited they are.
Honestly I'm quite excited too now, which I'm surprised about myself.
Getting to the coach I realise we don't get to choose where we sit, and the teachers have made a life of who's sitting where.
I suppose it's so nobody messes around, Gabriel is more than embarrassed when he has to sit next to a girl, but he tries to act cool.

'Noah, third seat from the back' Mr radwell says, pointing to the back of the coach,

I don't know why the teachers have made a whole picture chart of where people are, and aren't sitting surely sitting next to somebody you don't want to will cause more problems.

Chapter two

Walking to my seat and sitting down, I realise I'm sitting next to Ollie, the new boy from our class who Gabriel and Max were mocking for being 'gay' when they don't even know the guy to know his sexuality.

I think he feels intimidated by me, because of my friend's group, most probably when I sit next to him he puts his headphones in and looks out of the window, and that's how he stays for the whole two hours.

Getting my phone out from my pocket, i have a message from Gabriel,

09:01   Having fun over there?

I look towards him and can see him smirking, looking at his phone 'pathetic'
When we arrive, Mr Radwell is standing by the dorms, reading out names for who are sleeping in which dorm room.

'Noah, room eight'

Walking into the room I'm sharing with Jacob, and the new boy Ollie, at least it will be semi quiet. I feel bad for whoever is sharing with Grabiel or Max, or even worse, both of them together.

The room has one bunk bed, a single bed, and a small toilet area. Ollie has already taken the top bunk, and Jacob is laying across the single bed like a starfish, so I guess that means I'm taking the bottom bunk.

At ten o'clock, the teachers came around to turn the lights out. I know the last time I had to go to bed this early, but I knew I wouldn't be going to sleep anytime soon.

To make the situation even worse, Jacob is asleep within ten minutes and is snoring like a steam train. I put my headphones in and pull the pillow over my head, but I can still very slightly hear him.

I thought sharing with Jacob and Ollie would be quiet because they're both pretty quiet boys normally, but Jacob's snoring is definitely not quiet.

'How is anybody supposed to sleep with the sound of his snoring?' I hear Ollie from above me
'Honestly, I have no idea!'

Getting up from the bed, i shake Jacobs shoulder,

'Jacob, wake up!' i shout

He must be in a really deep sleep, because he doesn't even move, and just lets out an even bigger snore than before, turning to look at Ollie. He has pulled the quilt up over his face and is laughing into it.

I spend most of the night chatting with Ollie, and trying to sleep with headphones in to try and slightly block out the sound, and even my music on eighty percent isn't fully working. Speaking with Ollie and getting to know him during the night, he seems like a really nice guy. I feel almost guilty about Gabriel and Max saying mean things about him. They really shouldn't judge someone before knowing them.

'Right, line up boys and girls' Mr green the PE teacher shouts

Today is cross-country and if I was excited, I would be lying. Running through a muddy field in the pouring rain isn't something I enjoy, not only me, I think I'm speaking for the whole of year eleven.

By the end, we are all absolutely covered in mud, soaked through and freezing cold.

Laying on my bed that evening,

'Is there any way you can stop snoring so loud?' i say to Jacob,
'Is it really that bad?' he says, almost shocked.

Surely he knows how bad it is, it is really, really bad! I think the dorm next door could also hear him.

The next couple of nights went pretty much the same, laying awake, talking to Ollie, and sleeping the best I could while wearing headphones, which wasn't very much at all.

By the fourth night, I think I had just come to the realisation that I wasn't going to be sleeping until I got home. I'm pretty sure Ollie felt the same because I could hear him shuffling in the bed above me all night. I think I heard him sigh a few times, too.

I decided it wasn't even worth trying to sleep, and I would just watch movies all night. Instead, I might even fall asleep watching. That would be super helpful.

'Do you want to come and watch a movie with me?' I asked Ollie,

i thought if we were going to suffer these next few nights we may as well do it together.

' *'Yeah, sure'* he says, quickly getting down from the top bunk and sitting on mine.

I wake up a few hours later, the iPad still on my lap. Ollie is asleep with his head on my shoulder while I'm leaning against the bed headboard.

I should probably wake him up but that would just be horrible. Jacob is snoring even louder tonight, and I didn't even think that was possible.

I just lay in the same position, scrolling through my phone until Ollie wakes up.

'I'm so sorry, i fell asleep'
'Don't worry, we were both really tired'

He really didn't need to apologise, but it's sweet that he did.

'Same again tonight?' i ask
'Sure, sounds good'
I'm glad I'm getting to share a room with somebody who wants to stay up to watch movies and chat with me, if not I would have had some very long, boring nights alone.
Choosing a movie to watch, i decide on a horror and get ready for Ollie to come and join me, coming down from his bed and sitting down on mine he shuffles back and leans against the wall, he's wearing grey jogging bottoms and a green hoodie, i can't help but stare at him.

'*A horror… isn't that a bit scary'* Ollie says, after looking at the iPad screen,
'That's the point!' i laugh

I think Ollie spends most of the time hiding behind a pillow and at one point he got so scared he grabbed my hoodie string and pulled it so hard he almost strangled me.
Ollie demanded we watch a comedy after so he wasn't scared to go to bed alone, but during watching that i must have fallen asleep because the next thing i remember is waking up four hours later, one leg hanging off the bed, my iPad still playing on the floor.
I turn over in bed to grab my phone from under the pillow, where I always keep it but I'm face to face with Ollie, laying asleep next to me, staying as still as I possibly can trying not to wake up and hoping Jacob doesn't wake up anytime soon.
He looks so peaceful, his hand tucked under the pillow and the quilt up around his neck, why am I sitting here staring at him? If he was to wake up he would think I'm really weird.
Jacob sits up on his bed, and looks over to me laying on my back trying not to move a muscle,

'Why's he in your bed Noah?' he says looking confused.
'He must have fallen asleep when we were watching a movie'
''Why are you watching movies in bed together?' He says now looking like he's judging me, which he probably is,
'*Because we can't sleep with your really loud snoring, that's why Jacob!'*

I don't think he realises how bad it really is, when i say its loud that is no exaggeration. If I ever go on a residential trip again I'll make sure to tell the teachers I definitely do not want to share a room with Jacob!
He is a really good friend to me, and I thought it would be good for me to share with him, but his snoring is extreme.

'I'm going for breakfast, you coming?' Jacob asks as hes walking towards the door

I carefully try and get up off the bed to not wake Olli but that didn't work, as i'm pulling my hoodie on i hear Ollie moving on the bed,

'Whats the time?' He asks in a sleepy voice while rubbing his eyes,
'Its eight-thirty, you don't have to get up yet if you're still tired' I reply, smiling.
'Sorry i fell asleep again'
'It's ok, I know you were scared of the horror film so you didn't want to go to bed really' i say jokingly.
Jacob left the room for breakfast because i was taking too long to get ready, and he was starving apparently, i sit back down on the edge of the bed and look towards Ollie,

'So we are going home tomorrow' i say, almost feeling sad
'Yeah, at least we get to sleep in our own bed!' he replies

I feel almost hurt by that, I don't know why but maybe it's because I kind of enjoyed sharing my bed and just laying and watching movies until we fell asleep, of course I would never tell Ollie that.

'Come on, lets go get breakfast' i say poking him in the side as i'm about the stand up,
'Ol! What was that for!' He grabs onto my arm with one hand and uses the other to tickle me.
'Too bad i'm not ticklish' I laugh,
We both sit just looking at each other for what feels like a whole minute, ive never felt attracted to anyone before, but there is something about Ollie, something that makes me feel warm and happy.

In all honesty, this week hasn't been too bad which i didn't think i would ever say, sporting during the day. I can't say I enjoy sports much,but it's been fun.
Hanging out with friends, well Ollie, and watching late night movies, that was my favourite part! I think overall it's been a pretty good week.
The final night goes pretty much the same as every other night this week, listening to Jacob snoring and watching a movie until I fell asleep.
Of course Ollie joined, falling asleep before me for somebody who says he can't fall asleep easily. He is normally asleep within half an hour, while I lay awake for hours.
And as I predicted, I put on a movie, laying down to watch, and Ollie was asleep before we were even a quarter the way through.
Instead of watching the movie I turn to face ollie who is lying against the wall, he has one hand between his cheek and the pillow, and the other almost touching my face.
I shuffle a little closer, and pull the duvet up to my chin and just lay in the quiet, it's quite peaceful.
Just as I'm falling asleep, I feel Ollie move in his sleep, he shuffles closer to me, so our bodies are almost touching, and puts his arm over me so his arm is around my neck, and his hand touches the back of my head.
This is probably not ideal, especially since we are sharing a room with my friend who could wake and see at any minute, but am I going to move him? No, of course I'm not.

Chapter three

The next morning I woke up still laying in the same position I fell asleep, except now Ollie's face is almost touching mine, one hand above his head touching the headboard, and the other around my waist, with his knee up over mine.
Ollie open his eyes at looks at me,

'*Good morning*' he says with a massive smile on his face,
Morning, did you sleep ok?'
'I slept great' he replies, his hand still touching my waist.

While i felt happy, an warm and i loved this i was also scared i like Ollie that's clear, but i don't think i can date a boy even if i wanted to

'We better get up, the coach is leaving in an hour' i say, sitting up on the bed

Ollie sits up and looks at me and for a minute i'm lost in his eyes, he leans forward and kiss me on the lips, i quickly lean back and stand up,

'I'm so sorry, i thought you liked me too' he says looking down at his hands

I do like Ollie, I like him a lot! But I could never let him know that Gabriel and Max would make my life a living hell if they knew I was dating a boy and I don't need that right now, and instead of saying anything about the kiss, I get up, grab my bag and leave the room.
The kiss was great, and I felt so much connection with Ollie but this cannot happen, however much I want it too.
As i walk outside the dorm gabriel is standing outside on his phone,

'Alright Gabriel' i say, hoping he didnt hear anything that was just said back in the room,
'Alright mate' He replies looking up from his phone for a second.
'Are you going back to the coach now?'
'Yeah, i'll be there in a minute'

Walking away and making my way towards the coach, I can see Mr Radwell shouting names to get everybody on to the coach in some kind of order, if you can call it that , they are all just standing around shouting and pushing to get on because it's so cold.
I slept most the journey home, having only ten hours sleep all week well and truly caught up with me.
When we arrive back at school I can see mum sitting in the car waiting for me, I walk over and throw my bag on to the back seat and get into the car.
Mum leans over and give me a massive hug,

'Noah, I've missed you!'
'I've missed you too mum' i say smiling
'Have you had a good week?'
'Yeah, it's been really good'

Now we are back home, i have to be ready for monday morning at school with Narla thinking im her boyfriend, well technically i am but that doesnt mean i want to be.
I know if i told her i didn't want to be with her, Gabriel would have something to say about it, i mean he could always date her himself but everybody who knows Gabriel knows that would never happen.
Maybe we should try to set him up with somebody, and then he might realise it's strange and annoying, he was not going to give up until i had a girlfriend, a girlfriend i didn't even want and now i'm stuck in this situation because i'm too worried about hurting Narla, and being on bad terms with Garbiel.

Monday morning soon arrives, the weekends seem to go so fast when you're dreading something, and i was right to dread it as i walk into the school entrance i can hear Gabriel before i can even see him,

'Noah, your girlfriends here mate shes been waiting for you'

Oh for god sake! I need to just tell her, and him i don't want this.

'Hey Noah' Narla says which throwing her arms around my neck,
'Hey' i reply bluntly
'I've missed you so much'

She leans forward to kiss me, but pretending i didnt no she was about to do that, i turn my head to look away.

'Go on, give your girlfriend a kiss, what are you scared of?' Gabriel says
'Just leave it' i say, walking away.

I will have to deal with it later, he won't accept that i didn' kiss her in front of him,, like he needs proof or something.
It's not like i havent kissed her before, i have lots of times not that i enjoyed it, it didn't feel like when Ollie kissed me, but i have done it!
Mum says it will feel right when I meet the right girl and Narla obviously isn't the right girl for me, if not I would feel this spark that everybody in the school speaks about when kissing their girlfriends and boyfriends.
Slowly making my way to my next lesson I walk into the classroom and sit in my seat next to Ollie. I'm glad I don't have to sit anywhere near Gabriel or Max, they sit on the opposite side of the room to me.

'Hey Ollie'

He just looks at me with a sport of half-smile

'Are you ok?' i ask

Again he doesn't say anything, something must be going on, but it's not really my place to be pushing him to tell me his problems, but I guess it is my problem if this is because he kissed me, and I just got up and left him in the room.

It's been two weeks since Ollie was acting weird in class and not really speaking to me. I thought since the trip we were friends, but I can't really blame him for not wanting to be friends with me. I would be annoyed if somebody did the same to me.
Leaving the classroom at lunchtime Gabriel comes behind me and throws his arm around my shoulder,

'So do you like sitting next to Ollie? Is he gay then?'
'I don't know, how would i know, we don't even talk really'
'Well you sit next to him'
'Like i said, we don't speak really'

Gabriel and Max laugh at each other, I'm not sure why Gabriel is so interested in Ollie, he's always asking questions, maybe he secretly likes Ollie, maybe that's why he doesn't like speaking to girls for himself.
The thought of Gabriel liking Ollie makes me angry. I know it's not going to happen but the thought is enough to really annoy me.
Back at home that evening, I log on to my laptop and click on Instagram, scrolling through most of the posts are my friends taking selfies, and sharing posts about celebrities.
Clicking on the search bar, 'i wonder if Ollie has Instagram' i think to myself, maybe i can send a message, maybe he would feel more comfortable telling me what's been going on through message.
Typing his name in, his profile pops up, a picture of him and im guessing his mum he looks happy, happier than he ever does at school, i don't think anybody is really happy at school, but he looks really really unhappy.
Tapping out the message, i don't want him to think i'm invading his privacy i've literally searched him up on social media and sent him a private message.

08:22pm   'Hey Ollie, i hope you don't mind me messaging, i just wanted to check that you're ok? You seem really off at school lately'

I hold my finger over the screen for a few minutes before tapping send and putting my phone face down on the bed. A few hours pass and a notification comes through on my phone, opening the Instagram app, i see the message is from Ollie.

11:13pm   'Hi, you don't need to message to see if im ok, but honestly i'm not ok, i'm far from ok'

Staring at my phone, what does he mean by that? Has something happened at school? At home? Have I done something to upset him?'

11:21pm   'What's wrong? Do you want to speak about it?'

I lean back on the pillows on my bed, what could possibly have happened to make him feel this upset? I start to worry a little in case it's something I have done.
Another message comes through, opening it quickly and staring at the screen,

11:43pm   'Im fine, really, you don't need to worry about my problems, i just want to say though.. You need to rethink your friend group!'

What the hell does that mean? What's my friend group got to do with it? I know they can be idiots but I've never even seen them go near Ollie, let alone speak to him, they only speak about him.. Which i no isn't much better.
The next day at school i walk towards Gabriel and Max sitting on the wall outside the maths block,

'Hey, do you know what's going on with Ollie?' i ask
'What do you mean?' he replies with a smirk on his face
'I sent him a message on Instagram last night and.....'

Before i get to finish my sentence, Gabriel steps a little closer to me,

'Why would you message him on Instagram? Are you best friends now? Or do you fancy him'
'Because he's been acting really weird! And i have to sit next to him in class'
'Maybe he just fancies you' he laughs
'Don't be so stupid! He said something like i should rethink my friend group, what does that mean?'

By now Gabriel is looking a little uncomfortable, tapping his foot and just looking anywhere but at me.

'Do you fancy him Gabriel? Is that why you say horrible things about him?'
'What! No! Of course I don't like him, I'm not gay, that's disgusting!'

Why is being anything but straight disgusting to Gabriel? And why is he being so defensive? If he wont tell me, I'll try and get it out of Ollie! Getting my phone from my pocket i type out a message.

11:57am   'Meet me in the library at lunch'

Chapter four

It's not really my place to know what's going on in his life, but i would like to know why he says i need to rethink my friend group at least, Sitting in the library waiting to see if he is even going to turn up, i mean he didn't reply to my message to say he is coming or not.
I sit and wait around fifteen minutes, and just as I'm about to get up to leave he walks into the library and slumps himself on the floor next to me.
Running his hands through him hair aggressively, i can see he's stressed,

'So what's going on?' i ask
'I already told you not to worry. I don't know why you wanted me to meet you here, like you even care. You don't even know me' he says, looking like he's about to cry.
'I do care, especially if it's something my friends have done, or even worse, me!'
'Fine, its Gabriel' he says, almost shouting

I was taken by surprise. Are they secretly seeing each other? A knot forming in my stomach,

'What about Gabriel?' i ask, almost not wanting to know

He looks at me blankly like i should already know,

'What about Gabriel? You should know he's your friend, he's the biggest bully in the whole school!'

So they aren't seeing each other. I dont no why but I'm feeling relieved about that answer, of course it's awful that Gabriel is bullying Ollie, but I'm glad they are not in a secret relationship.

'Hes bullying you?' i ask, a concerned tone in my voice
'Yeah, really bad! He has been for a while now'

By now he has full tears running down his cheeks, I knew Gabriel was a massive idiot a lot of the time and he says things to make me feel a bit crap, but I never thought they could make someone feel this low.
I put my arm around his shoulder and pull him in for a hug,

'Do you want me to speak to him?' i ask
'NO! That would make things even worse, him knowing im meeting and speaking with his friends'
'Has he hurt you?' i ask, rubbing my hand on my his shoulder
No, it's all been verbal'

'I won't say anything, but you have to promise me, you will tell me if it gets more than verbal ok?'

'Ok, promise' he nods and smiles, putting his hand up and his pinky finger out towards mine, we both laugh, I put my pinky finger to join him.

'Pinky promise'

Pushing my hands to the floor to stand up and walking towards the door, Ollie runs behind me and hugs me one more time, he felt like he really needed that hug.

'Thanks Noah, im glad your nothing like your friends'
'Well I'm glad too!' i say laughing

I'm glad I can be a good friend to Ollie. He seems like he really needs it. Maybe not one who is best friends with the person who is bullying him, but he knows that I would never do anything to upset him.
I really wanted to say something to Gabriel, but I promised Ollie I wouldn't, sitting in my maths class, looking up from my work, I could see Gabriel glaring over at me. What is he looking at? Does he know I was speaking to Ollie in the library?

'Noah, come here!' Gabriel says as i'm leaving the classroom
'Yeah, what's up?'

I can't even look at him the same way, knowing he made someone so miserable, someone who had done nothing at all to him, someone as lovely as Ollie.

'You coming to mine this weekend? Narla is coming' he asks
'Na, im busy mate, sorry'
'Your never busy on the weekends, you've got to put time in to see your girlfriend, or it will never work!'
'Maybe.. Just maybe I don't want it to work, maybe I don't want a girlfriend, you could always date her yourself! It felt so good to get that out!
'Na, come on mate
'She likes you, not me!'
'Well maybe i don't like her' that sounded way worse than it should have.

I don't want to hurt Narla's feelings, but why should I date somebody just because my friend tells me too? Of course the weekend comes and i go round to Gabriels, more because i want to see if he says anything about Ollie, and to my surprise he does.

'So, that new boy Ollie, I found out he is gay!' he says, sounding proud of himself

Ok, so what? Why does it matter? Especially to Gabriel, what does anybody's sexuality have to do with him in any way shape, or form.

'How did you find out?' i ask, curious as to what he is going to say
'He told me, didn't he'
'When do you even speak to him Gabriel?'
'Why are you trying to protect him? Do you fancy him? Are you gay too?'

By now, everybody in the room is laughing, but I'm so angry I don't even care that they are laughing at me.

'No Gabriel, I'm not gay! But i dont no why you think it's cool to be mean to people all the time!'
'Ok, ok, chill out mate'

Maybe he will stop being mean now, and Ollie will be ok at school from now on, but with Gabriel you never know.
It used to be Gabriel and Max spending all day, everyday together, but since Max got a girlfriend, he isn't around as often and I think Gabriel is a bit sad about that, and that's why he's taking it out on other people, but that isn't an excuse.
He was the one who set him up with his girlfriend, so it's partly his fault, anyway.

It's Sunday evening, and I'm sitting in my room doing my homework, because as well as being late every day, I'm also terrible at doing homework on time too. it's due tomorrow and I have barely made a start.
I think it's probably because I spend more time watching TV than actually doing any writing. It's past midnight before I actually finished checking my phone one last time before I go to sleep, and I have a message from Ollie he sent three hours ago. How did I not hear it?
Now he's going to think I'm ignoring him because I didn't hear my stupid phone.
It's probably too late to reply now, he's most likely sleeping but I should reply so he doesnt think I just didn't want to speak to him.

09:20pm   'I really don't want to go to school tomorrow' Ollie wrote
12:38am   'If you don't want to spend lunch alone, we can go and sit in the library if you like?'

To my suprise, he replies pretty quickly,

12:42am   'Yeah, that would be nice'

I really like spending time with Ollie, he is much nicer than my friends, and I feel like we have a really good connection, a connection I don't feel with Narla.

'NOAH!' i hear being shouted down the corridor the next morning, i turn to look towards Gabriel and Max,

'Yeah' i say bluntly
'At lunchtime we are meeting on the field, you need to come and speak to Narla'
'Yeah, i can't today i have to stay in and do last weeks homework i missed'

I'm lying of course, but i can't exactly say "i can't, im meeting Ollie"

'Tonight then, at mine?'
'Ok, see you then'

I don't really want to go, but I also don't want to have to explain why. Maybe this is my chance to actually tell Narla I don't want to be with her. I know it won't go down well but I have to do what's right for me for once.

Ollie is in the library before me today, walking towards him and sitting down he looks at me,

'I didn't think you were coming'
'I'm only five minutes late' i laugh
Thanks for coming to sit with me i really appreciate it'
'You don't need to thank me, that's what friends are for' I smile.

He looks down at his lap, looking a little sad but I think nothing of it. He's had a lot going on in the last few weeks, I don't want to put more pressure on by asking questions.
I'm glad i can sit with Ollie at lunch times so he doesn't have to sit alone worrying that Gabriel is going to walk in, it would be worse for me if he did come in anyway i'm sure he wouldn't even say a thing to Ollie, he would be wondering why i'm in the library instead of with them.

Arriving at Gabriel's later that day, I really wish I had just stayed at home. They are just sitting around playing video games on the Xbox. It seems a little pointless to just sit here and do nothing, it always seems pointless.
One good thing about the whole thing is that Narla didn't come over, so i didn't have to deal with that.

I have found myself meeting Ollie most lunchtimes, and I must say it's much nicer than sitting on the field having to deal with Gabriel and Max being massive idiots.
I never thought i would be saying i enjoy sitting in the library, before i met Ollie, i had barely stepped foot in the library.
Gabriel always asks where I'm going, or what I'm doing. I always tell him I'm just doing school work, and he seems to believe it.
I have actually been spending less and less time with my friends, I still have to see Narla occasionally of course, she still thinks we are together, it's now been six months and she still thinks we are a couple because I'm too much of a wimp to end things.

Chapter five

Ollie didn't even know i had a girlfriend, not until one afternoon we were standing in the corridor, early for our english lesson, i no i was early! There is a first time for everything! I was standing facing Ollie when Narla ran to me, hugging me from behind.
Turning around to look at her, she was with all her friends,

'H..Hey Narla'
'Hey, I've missed you so much! We need to hang out soon' she says, laying her head on my chest and crossing her arms over my back.

By now Ollie is looking really confused, he didn't think i even had a crush, let alone a girlfriend, just as she was about to leave she leant in and kissed me on the lips, reluctantly i kissed her back, not because i wanted to, but because all her friends where standing glaring at me.
By now Ollie is just staring at me, and if i'm honest I feel a little silly.

'I didn't know you had a girlfriend' he asks in a surprised tone
'Yeah, Gabriel set us up six months ago, and it's kind of just never ended'
'Are you happy with her?'
'Not really, i don't really like her that way, i just feel bad telling her' i say, shaking my head
You need to tell her Noah'
'I know, and i will'

Gabriel comes walking down the corridor like he owns the place, I can see Ollie is getting really nervous, he's looking at the floor, and twiddling his thumbs.

'Alright Noah?' he says nudging my arm with his elbow

Then he walks towards Ollie, he looks at me as if to say "help"
'Alright Ollie' he says ruffling his hair

Ollie stays silent just looking down towards the floor, I feel so bad he shouldn't have to feel like this, it's not fair, I wanted to say something so badly but I promised Ollie I would keep quiet.

'When are you seeing Narla again then Noah?' he says, throwing his arm around my shoulder.
'I just saw her a while ago'
'Did you kiss her?' he asks me, then looking at ollie
Did he kiss her Ollie?'

Ollie just nods his head, not saying a word

'Good lad Noah!' he smiles

Good lad? Why is he talking like he's a relationship expert! Turning to walk away from us, he slaps Ollie over the back of the head, and it wasn't a small slap, I hear it standing on the other side of the door to him.
I can't not say anything, why should ollie suffer in silence?

'Why did you hit him like that?' i ask clearly sounding annoyed

Ollie is now looking at me, half scared, half confused. I know I promised I wouldn't say anything, but I can't just let Gabriel get away with it, someone has to stand up to him.

Why do you care so much Noah? Do you fancy him? Is that why you don't want to be with Narla we all know you don't like her really'
'No I don't Gabriel, I have a girlfriend.. Remember the girlfriend you forced me to be with'

By now we have a bit of an audience, I think they think there's going to be a fight, the people in this school are like leeches when they think a fight is going to break out.
Everybody stands around shouting "fight, fight" and run in one direction, this time they didn't get a fight to watch, Gabriel ended up walking away. I'm not saying I wouldn't have fought him, I would have kicked his arse.
I walk in to the classroom and Ollie is already sitting down,

'Are you ok?' i ask
'Yeah, i'm good'

I know he's not good, nothing is good about what Gabriel is doing, it's not fair.

'You sure you're ok?' i ask again, maybe hoping he will admit that he really isn't ok
'Yeah, you don't need to stick up for me, I can handle it!' he replies, sounding annoyed.

I know right now, he cannot handle it, but I don't want to say that and make him feel even worse.

'Do you want to skip this lesson?' i ask with a smile

He looks up at me shocked, pulling out his phone to check the time

'Ok, are you sure?'
'Yeah, come on quickly before everybody gets here'
'What about Gabriel? Won't he wonder where you are?'
'I don't care what Gabriel thinks'

We both laugh, and quickly leave the classroom, running down the corridor to the caretakers cupboard.
I have skipped lessons here lots of times, nobody has ever checked her, most people hide in the toilets, or the back of the field, but they always get caught.
Sitting on the floor, surrounded by mops and antibacterial spray bottles,

'Are you sure you want to skip the lesson?' Ollie asks sounding worried
'I've done this loads of times' i laugh
Sometimes when I want to just sit and think on my own, or if somebody is really annoying me, normally Gabriel.

'You know Noah, you're really amazing!' Ollie says, tilting his head towards my shoulder

Shocked, i sat in silence for a few minutes just looking at him,

Sorry, I shouldn't have said that' he says, looking upset.

'No it's ok, you're my friend, I'll always stick up for you' I smile.

A few days later, Ollie didn't come in to our english lesson which was weird, because i didn't think he would skip a lesson alone, and he was in the lesson before break i normally spend breaks and lunch with him, but i had to go and see Mr Radwell about being late again that morning.
Mrs Milling the head teacher comes in to our classroom,

'Gabriel Morley, my office now!'

What the hell is going on? Why is Ollie not here, and why is Gabriel being called into the head teachers office?
Looking over at Max,

'What's happened?' i whisper
'Gabriel had a fight at break, it was pretty bad'
'A fight? With who?'
'Ollie'

My stomach drops, Ollie wouldn't fight Gabriel, he was terrified of him,
I can just about hear Max talking to others in the class about the fight, just about making out what he's saying. It sounded like it was Gabriel beating Ollie up, not fighting at all.

At lunch i walk into my form room and slump down in to my chair

'Mr Radwell, where is Ollie?'
'I think he's gone home Noah'
'And Gabriel?'
'He's in the office waiting for his parents to come and collect him, hes had been excluded'

It must have been pretty bad for him to be excluded, and for Ollie to be sent home one person who will know exactly what happened is Max, he is spending much more time with Gabriel now that he and his girlfriend broke up.

'Hey max, what actually happened?' i ask walking towards him in the corridor
They had a fight, like i said' he says
'Was it bad? Was Ollie really hurt?
'His mouth was bleeding pretty bad'

Walking away and taking myself to the caretaker's cupboard again, I've found this kind of a comfort place for me, which sounds really weird but it's a good place to be alone.
Getting my phone from my coat pocket i type out a message to Ollie

01:52pm   'Are you ok? I'm so sorry this happened x'

He didn't reply, in fact i didn't hear a thing from him all week, he didn't reply to my messages and he wasn't in school.
When he did come back the following week, I could finally see what Gabriel had actually done to him. He still had a cut across the top of his lip, it was slightly swollen and red, and he also had a big bruise across his cheek bone.
I knew it was going to be bad, but not this bad. I knew Gabriel was also back at school today and it felt like my job to protect Ollie, it was going to be really hard for him.

'If you ever want to skip a lesson, just let me know' i say with a hand on Ollie's shoulder

It's probably not a good idea to keep skipping lessons, with our GCSE's coming up , but I can revise at home after school and on the weekends.
I can tell Ollie is nervous, and I don't blame him. I'm feeling even worse than I was before about all of this, I just want everything to stop and be good for him.
Gabriel hasn't said a word to Ollie since he came back to school, i don't think he would be that stupid again, but with Gabriel you never know, he likes to
surprise.
The school holidays are coming up, it will be good to get away from here for a week. There has been so much drama in the last few weeks. I knew the last year of school would be stressful but this is stressful to a whole new level.
Gabriel has tried to speak to me a couple of times but to be honest I don't want to speak to him. I know we have been friends for six years, but he can't keep treating people so badly and thinking he can get away with it.

<u>Chapter six</u>

Ollie has been keeping his distance too, but I think that's because he's scared about what Gabriel will say if he sees us together. I'm not worried about that but I want to respect Ollie and do what he feels is right at the minute.

Since the trip, we have become really good friends, probably more like best friends. Actually he is one of the only people i trust, he is one of the most amazing people i've met, ever. Sitting on the bench outside, scrolling through my phone and eating a sausage roll I had just brought from the school canteen, Gabriel and Max walked towards me.

'What do you want?' i say, taking a bite from my sausage roll
'Why are you sticking up for Ollie and not your friends?'
'FRIENDS! I can't be friends with people who beat others up for doing nothing wrong!'

By now, Gabriel is closer to me, almost in my face

'Protecting your boyfriend?' he laughs
'Gabriel, why don't you get a life!'
'He's not denying it, is he?' he says, looking towards Max for approval.

By now we are getting a crowd around us expecting a fight to happen,

'He's not my boyfriend! I just don't like that you are mean to him, there's no need for it, but even if he was my boyfriend that would have nothing to do with you!'

Getting more and more angry the more Gabriel speaks, and wanting to punch him to shut him up, but then again i don't want to be expelled from school, that would be really bad and my parents would be so angry, especially my dad if he ever found out it was a boy i was fighting over.
The next thing I know I'm being pushed backwards, falling onto the table behind me, everyone standing around cheering like they're at a football match and their favourite team just scored a goal.
Stumbling back to my feet, I swung my arm and punched Gabriel in the mouth. God that felt so good! He hit me back a couple of times, but by now I'm sitting on him, punching him repeatedly in the face. This is until a group of teachers come running out to break it up.
Of course I'm scared about what's going to happen next, but it just felt so good to hit him, like all the anger I've built because of him all came out at once.

'Noah, office now!' My radwell shouts across at me,

This looks way worse on me, i was hitting him when the teachers came outside, but he was the one who started it. If he hadn't pushed me to start we would never have had a fight at all.

The school holidays have been so boring, I kind of wish I could go back to school. I never thought I would hear myself say I would rather be at school than at home.
I got expelled from school the week before the half term, of course my mum and dad were angry at me.
My mum even mentioned sending me to boarding school. She's been looking at all these posh schools on google and showing me them thinking I'll be interested in one of them.
I've made it clear i don't want to go, but apparently i have no choice and if that's
what they choose, that's where i'll go.
Sitting in my room and leaning to pick up my phone from the desk next to my bed i tap out a message to Ollie,

12:43pm   'My mum and dad are thinking of sending me to boarding school'

I don't want to go to boarding school. I can't think of anything worse, Ollie quickly replies to my message.

12:51pm   'what? Because of the fight?'
12:54pm   'yeah, but just so you know it wasn't my fault!'

I didn't even know he knew i had a fight, he wasn't around when it happened but then news travels fast around that school, and he would have noticed i wasn't at school all week.

Every time i tell mum i don't want to go, she says her and dad made the decision, but when i ask dad if i can stay at St Mildens high he just kind of grunts and says nothing, i know this is all my mums decision, because my dad doesn't care about anything i do, the only time he says anything to me is to ask if i have a girlfriend yet, or when I'm going too.

The first day back seemed to go pretty well. I had to sit in the same classroom as Gabriel, but he didn't say anything to me, which I was glad about.
At lunch time me and Ollie sat in the canteen, it was a hot summer day and normally i would sit outside in the sun, but i didn't want to bump into Gabriel, and Max, not because i was scared, because i'm not but because i don't want to get excluded again.
Ollie slams his hand down on the table while looking directly at me

'So, do you still have to move to boarding school?'
'Yeah i think so, my mum is making me look around one on Saturday'
'Do you want to go there?'
No, I want to stay here! But my mum wont let me do that'
'Who will i sit with and eat lunch with everyday, and who will i skip lessons with?' he giggles
'You'll have to make a new friend' I replied, raising my eyebrows at him.

We both laugh, the first time i laughed since my mum told me she was making me move, ive tried to think of every single way i can get out of going, like maybe i can just act like a really horrible person when i go to look around, and they won't want me in their perfect school, but then she would just find a different one for me, or maybe i can just join every single after school club in this school, she's always telling me i should.

Saturday morning arrives much to my disappointment, walking into my mum's bedroom and sitting on the end of her bed, she can probably guess what I'm going to say, I can tell when she looks at me and shakes her head side to side.

'Do i really have to go, i want to stay here with my friends'
'Your friends where Gabriel and Max, Noah and i don't think they are you friends anymore'
'I have a new friend, i haven't been hanging around with Gabriel and Max for ages now'
'Whos this new friend?' she asks sounding like she's shocked that i have actually made a new friend,
'His name is Ollie, he's really nice'

Mum just nods while looking down at her phone, she's been acting so excited all morning about looking around this school, it seems almost like she's trying to get rid of me and the fight was just an excuse.
Just as we are about to leave, i get a message from Ollie,

10:01am   'Hey, I thought I would just say good luck while looking around the new school today!'

Good luck? Is he trying to get rid of me as well? Arriving at the new school, from outside, it looks like an old church. There are a bunch of students sitting on the wall outside. The uniform is a lot different to my navy blazer, white shirt and black trousers that i wear now, The boys are wearing a green coloured pair of shorts, white shirts and a checked blazer, the girls wearing pretty much the same except with a skirt.

'The uniforms looks nice, don't you think Noah?' mum says with a smile
'Nice??' I look at her with a frown.

The principal of the school walks over to meet us, she is a stern looking lady with her hair tightly tied back in a ponytail, she shakes mums hand first and then mine.

Nice to meet you Noah, im Mrs Becking'

Looking around the school, it looks even bigger on the inside than the outside. There are lots of students standing around the hallways looking at me as I walk through the school, mum is speaking with Mrs Becking and asking a lot of questions while I'm just slowly walking behind them.

Back in the car ready to make our way home, taking one of my headphones out and looking at mum,

'Please mum, don't make me go there'
'I thought it was a lovely school, why don't you like it?'
'I don't want to move to a new school, i like my school now'

Mum turns the engine on and begins to drive, the entire drive home we sit in silence, i think she's just upset because she really wanted me to like it.
Walking through the front door at home, Dad asks how it went but instead of answering i go straight upstairs to my room.
Slumping back on my bed and pulling the quilt up over my head so many thoughts going through my head, why do I have to move when I didn't even cause the fight and Gabriel admitted that! Why boarding school? Don't my parents want me at home and the fight is just an excuse? I can feel myself starting to cry, pulling the pillow over my head and I scream into it.
Just as i do Dad walks in to the room

'Noah, are you ok?' he asks, looking at me with the pillow still in my hands,

Turning on to side, facing away from dad,

'*Of course I'm not ok!'*
'Your mum asked me to come and speak to you about the school'
'I don't want to speak about it'
'Noah, mum said you can stay at your school'
Quickly turning over and sitting up,

'What? She was desperate for me to move'
'She thought it was best, but she can see how unhappy its making you'

I think that was the most i have spoken to dad in about three years, as soon as he leaves my room i grab my phone and send Ollie a message letting him know that i'm not moving school now, i don't know what made my mum change her mind, but i'm so glad she did.
A little while later, Ollie replies ,

02.50pm   'OMG, I'm so happy for you x'
Since I met Ollie, I have been so much happier, it's so good having a friend who isn't like Gabriel and Max, a friend who doesn't just want to sit and speak about girls all day, everyday

Monday at school, i dont think ive ever been so happy to be going to school, I think since i thought i was going to be moving i'm going to be appreciating it a little more and work harder, at least mum won't have at least mum won't have any reason to move me again then.'

Chapter seven

Early for my lesson, I stand in the corridor by the classroom door, for once i'm the first person to arrive.
As i'm looking down at my timetable i hear somebody call my name,

'Noah!'

Looking up, I can see Ollie begins running towards me, when he gets a little closer he throws his arms out and around me.

'Im glad your not moving school Noah'
'Me too, i'm so happy' i reply

Ollie still has his arms around me when Gabriel and Max walk towards us down the corridor, noticing them he quickly lets go and moves away.
I notice them looking towards each other and saying something quietly as they walk towards me.

'Whats going on here then Noah?' Gabriel asks
'*Nothing is going on, what do you mean?'* i know exactly what he means
'Look like you two were hugging to me'
'So what? Why does it matter?'

Ollie is looking down at his phone but i can see a smile on his face, like hes happy ive just admitted to hugging him in public.

'What have you decided to be gay now like Ollie?'
'People don't just choose to be gay, Gabriel!'
By now I'm almost laughing at him, he has no idea!

'No, I'm not gay. Ollie was hugging me because I'm not moving to a new school now, but even if i was gay, that would also be none of your business'
'You were moving to a new school?' he asks, his tone now changed.
'Yeah, my mum was going to send me to boarding school because of the fight'

That was the first time I had spoken to Gabriel since the fight, I'm just glad it didn't end up as bad as last time. Maybe we can become friends again, not as good friends as before, but still civil.
At lunch time, deciding to go and sit with Gabriel and Max, I know it seems crazy after everything that has happened, but they are the friends I have known the longest.

Ollie seems a bit off with me in the lesson after lunch, i no he doesn't have many friends, but i always let him know i'm his friend as well as theirs, hopefully with time i can make Gabriel and Max see that Ollie is actually cool, they should give him a chance.
Sitting in my seat next to Ollie, tapping my pen on the table.

'You ok?' i ask quietly

He looks towards me,

'Yeah, why wouldn't I be?'

I don't know what i've done wrong, or if this is because of lunch time but this is the first time Ollie has spoken to me like this, and i don't like it.

What's wrong?' i ask concerned,

He just looks at me, and then away again. Maybe I need to give him time to get over whatever he is upset about, which is probably me.

A couple of days later, Ollie still seems off with me, I don't understand why, we were really good friends before and now he's just ignoring me.
On the field at lunch with Gabriel, Max and Maddie, we are all sitting around talking and eating, Maddie nudges my shoulder,

'Noah, did you know your friend Ollie is dating Ellis now?'
'What? Since when? I ask clearly shocked
'I don't know, a week or so'
'I told you he was gay' Gabriel says, sounding really pleased with himself
'How do you know?' i ask Maddie
'Ellis is telling everyone, I'm surprised you haven't heard , I thought Ollie was your friend?'

I sit in science for the next few minutes before getting up and walking away without saying anything at all.
I guess I'm just confused as to why I'm feeling the way I am about Ollie having a boyfriend, we are just friends yet I'm feeling a mix of upset and jealousy.

I'm walking to school a few days later when i see Ellis walking ahead of me

'Ellis' i shout, hoping he will hear me over the music playing though his headphones
'Oh,.. hi Noah'
'How are you and Ollie?' I ask, secretly hoping he's going to say awful!
'We're really good actually, we are going on a proper date on Saturday'
'Oh, that will be nice, where are you going?'

'Just to the cinema, Ollie loves movies'

If I told Gabriel about this date, he would want to go to the cinema just to cause a problem. I know it would be really wrong of me to do that and ruin this for them, but that doesn't stop me, and of course I tell Gabriel.

'Gabriel, did you know Ellis and Ollie are going on a date on Saturday?'
'Really? Where are they going?'
'Ellis said the cinema'

Gabriel looks at Max and then back towards me,

'Should we go to the cinema too?' he says grinning
'Uh.. yeah, but we don't know what they are seeing or what time they are going'
'I will find all of that out, I'll speak to Ellis' he has an even bigger grin across his face now.

Gabriel is really good at getting information out of people without them thinking anything of it, plus Ellis is kind of their friend too as well as mine, just not so much in the last year, he made lots of new friends and just slowly started hanging around with us less.
Saturday arrives and i send a message to Gabriel to find out what's going on with the cinema trip,

09:06am   'Hey, what are we doing today? Are we going to the cinema?

He quickly replies with a time and place to meet, starting to feel nervous like Ollie would be thinking it is me that set this up, i mean technically it was me, but it was Gabriel that did all the planning.
Walking in the cinema, I can see we are the first people here, which is better than walking in when Ollie and Ellis are already here! The film trailers started and they still hadn't turned up.

'Noah, they're here' Max says, nudging my arm.
Looking down the stairs, I can see them walking up towards us. I'm not feeling even more nervous and pretend I'm looking down at my phone, looking for their seat. They sit down right in front of us. Gabriel looks towards me and smiles, clearly very happy with this situation.
We can just about hear what they are saying with the sound of the movie playing, Ellis looks back at us, and then back to Ollie

Do you want to move? We don't have to sit here'
No it's fine, we can stay here' he replies, forcing a smile.

I don't know why but I'm feeling really really bad, like I shouldn't have come here, now they are going to be on their date feeling they are being watched so they cant enjoy themselves.

Chapter eight

Technically they are being watched because I don't think Gabriel has even looked away from them once, I don't think he's even blinked!

When the movie finishes Gabriel suggests we follow them to see where they are going next, of course i dont think this is a good idea at all, and try to suggest we do something different that would be more fun than walking around, following those two on their date.

Gabriel always chooses what we do though, so who am I to argue and I kind of want to know where they are going.

After a full three hours of walking, I think after the first hour I was wishing we could just stop, they knew we were following them and it did look a little strange.

What am I even supposed to say about that if he asks why we followed, or how we even knew they were going on a date.

In my room that evening I started to regret ever going to the cinema, and making them feel uncomfortable. I wouldn't have liked it if it was me on that date, I wish it was me on that date not Ellis, but I would never say those words, those are thoughts for my head only.

Getting my phone out from my pocket, i send Ollie a message,

10:50pm	'Im so sorry about today'
10:55pm	'how did you know we were going to the cinema?'
10:59pm	'Gabriel knew, i don't know how'

I did know how, Ellis told me, and i told Gabriel, i hope he's not to mad at me, i mean who would blame him, he's just trying to have a date with his boyfriend, and then there's me and my friends following him around the whole time, i think anyone would be annoyed about that.

At school on Monday, now I have had a day to think about Saturday, and I realise how wrong it was. If I was any friend I would be happy for Ollie, but I'm not, I'm so far from happy and I don't know why.

Walking into my maths class, Ollie is already in his seat, sitting down next to him. I just smile, honestly I don't know what I'm supposed to say to him.

I don't want to make things even more awkward than they already are.

As i'm leaving the classroom, i feel a tap on my shoulder, turning around to face Ollie,

'Do you want to come and meet Ellis with me for lunch?' he asks

I can't exactly say no, but i dont want too, maybe he just feels sorry for me,

'Yeah, sure' i reply

Walking towards the canteen, already regretting my decision I should have just said I was meeting Gabriel and Max, Ollie walks and sits next to Ellis, leaving me sitting facing them both.

'Hi Noah' Ellis says , his hand on the table holding Ollies
'Hi' i reply, giving a slight smile
'Did you enjoy the cinema on Saturday?'

Ollie looks towards Ellis with an embarrassed look on his face, i'm just as embarrassed i can feel my cheeks burning, i don't reply to his question, just nodding my head to say 'yes' Making an excuse to leave, I quickly get up and leave the table and for the next couple of days I completely avoid both Ollie and Ellis, who both seem happier than ever, which is quite annoying.

At home that evening I must have been acting odd, because even mum noticed, and she never notices anything, like ever.

'What's wrong Noah? You seem sad' she says tapping her hand on the sofa next to her suggesting me to sit down,
'Nothing, im ok' i reply, sitting next to her
'Are you sure?'

I'm debating telling mum everything about Ollie and Ellis, it's just weird because not even i know why im feeling so annoyed they are together, so how can i expect anyone else to understand.

'It's just my friend Ollie, he has a new boyfriend'
'You don't like his boyfriend?' she tilts her head slightly while still looking at me,
'Yeah, we were friends before, i dont no, its just weird'

Mum puts her hand on top of mine,

'Do you like ollie?'
'Of course i like him, he's a really great friend to me'
'I mean more than a friend Noah, do you like him more than just a friend?' She says her hand is now stroking my hair.

I just sit and look down at my hands, I have felt confused before but never this confused. Do I like Ollie more than a friend? Is that why I'm so jealous of him with Ellis?

'*I think so*' i reply to mum, still looking down at my hands to not make eye contact
'*Then you need to tell him, let him know how you feel.*' she says, hugging me tightly.

Going up to my room, I try to build the courage to take mum's advice and send Ollie a message telling him everything.

10:11pm   'Hey Ollie, so firstly how are you? I wanted to tell you something, something I cannot say to your face, because we both know how I'm the WORST person for opening up about anything! Anyway, I know you're with Ellis, and that you're really happy but i like you, and i just wanted you to know'

Laying on my bed, I start to wonder if I did the right thing, will Ollie tell Ellis? Will they tell all of my friends? Or even worse, show them the message? I know Ollie, and I know he wouldn't do that, but what about if Ellis is with him now and sees it? I click on the Instagram app and on to my message I just sent to Ollie hoping I can quickly delete it before he has seen it, but it's too late, he is already typing.

10:33pm   'Why didn't you tell me before I got together with Ellis? I liked you, well i like you and i thought you knew that, i was so happy when we meeting for lunch everyday and skipping lessons together, but i thought you were straight and we were just friends, and that's when i met Ellis, he doesn't make me half as happy as you do though xx'

I read the message, and then reread it a few times with tears in my eyes, he thought i was straight, i also thought i was straight, but Ollie just changed me, he changed everything for me, i should have told him when i had the chance, before he and Ellis got together, i've known for months that i liked him. It started on the school trip, and it's been months since then. I should have said something before, I guess I was scared.

It's the school holiday, a whole six weeks off school. I think I need that, especially after finally telling Ollie how I feel about him, and it gives me time to think about everything. He said he likes me too, and has for a long time but he does have a boyfriend now and he can't just finish things with Ellis and hurt him, which I understand because it was the same with Narla.
That just shows what a kind person Ollie is and that's how similar we are. Sitting at the end of my bed, it's only the first day of the holidays and already I'm wondering what I should do. Mum did mention going to my nan and grandads but i kind of want to do something more fun, I don't know, meet some friends or something.
Sending Gabriel a message to see what he's doing today,

10:01am   'Hey Gabriel, are you free today?'
10:12am   'I have to go out with my mum and dad today, can we do something tomorrow?'
10:26am   'Yeah sure, sounds good!'

So Gabriel is busy, Max is on holiday in Turkey, and of course I would love to meet with Ollie but he said he promised to meet Ellis. They asked me to go alone with them, but I think that would just be weird, considering.
Although though my boredom, i start thinking i should just go for something to do,

Picking my phone up from the bed, I type out a message to Ollie but before I do I realise he's already messaged me first.

11:15am   'So, do you want to come with us today?'
11:22am   'Don't you think it would be weird? You know i like you, and i'm coming to meet you and your boyfriend'
11:26am   'No, I think it will be good! I really want to see you!'
11:31am   'I want to see you too, but could we not do it another time, when you're not meeting Ellis?'
11:41am   'we can do both, meet us at the shopping mall at one xx'

So i guess i'm going, and if i'm getting there by one i better get moving quickly, throwing on a pair of jeans and a t-shirt, ruffling my hair in the mirror as i leave the house.
I get to the mall and Ollie and Ellis are already standing by the door waiting for me. Ollie looks happy to see me, a huge grin across his face but Ellis looks annoyed, probably because of the cinema situation, but this time I was actually invited.
Walking around the mall, I stay behind Ollie and Ellis most of the time. They walk hand in hand , kissing every single time we stop for more than a second, almost like Ellis is trying to make me jealous, but for all he knows i'm the straight friend.

'Do you want to go to the cinema, Noah?' Ollie asks
Uh.. yeah, sure, if you want'

I don't think there is anything more awkward than going to the cinema with your current love interest and they're boyfriend. I sat at the end of the row next to Ellis, while he and Ollie spent the whole of the trailers Cuddling, kissing and holding hands.
He thinks I'm your typical straight boy, so I know he's not trying to make me jealous because why would I be? But I am, I really really am.
During the movie, I keep glancing at Ollie, and he just smiles, oh my god, I wish it was me with Ollie, why can't I be the one holding his hand? He looks just perfect, and even more perfect with the light of the cinema screen shining on his face.
I don't know what happens next, but Ellis pulls his phone out from his pocket, replies to a text message and then gets up and leaves the cinema, i look over towards Ollie and lean forward over the empty seat and whisper in his ear.

'Where has he gone?'
'His mum texted, family emergency apparently'

I lean back over and sit back in my seat, when Ollie gets up and sits in the seat next to me, I look towards him and smile, not wanting to look too comfortable in case Ellis walks back in again.

Just as i was getting in to the movie, which i thought was boring to start with, Ollie puts his hand on top of mine, i just frozen, i know i was wishing for this just half an hour ago, but now it's actually happening, i'm not sure what i'm supposed to do, i mean i have never fancied a boy before, let alone anything else.

I quickly move my hand out from under Ollies, he looks at me shocked, probably wondering why I have said I like him, but i don't want to hold his hand.

I move my arm up, and put it around his neck, pulling his head towards my chest, and hold onto his hand with my other hand.

If Ellis came back in now, I'm sure there would be a lot of trouble, but am I going to stop? No, I'm not.

Considering I have never even hugged a boy before, well apart from the one guy in year eight who I hugged because his pet fish had died, and he was so upset about it, but that was just because I felt really sorry for him.

But sitting here, hugging Ollie it feels normal, it feels good, he feels like home.

A few days after the cinema, and me falling for Ollie harder than i ever thought possible, i had planned to meet Gabriel and thought about inviting Ollie, but instead of going out i decided to invite them both round to my house,

Ollie arrived first, which is probably better than him walking in and Gabriel already being here, also i should have probably told them both the other was coming round too.

The doorbell rings, rushing downstairs to answer,

'Ollie!' i smile, hugging him tightly

Taking him upstairs, i had to tell him that Gabriel would also be joining us, which shouldn't be a problem really, i went out with him and his boyfriend, Gabriel is just a friend.

'Hey, so Ollie, Gabriel is going to be coming round soon too'
'What? Why didn't you tell me before?'
'Im sorry, i just really wanted you to come too'

I move closer to him, and put my arms around his neck, leaning in i whisper in his ear,

'Im sorry, don't be mad with me'

He turns his head slightly, looking into my eyes before leaning in and kisses me on the lips lightly, Leaning back slightly, still looking at him, before leaning in and kissing him again, this time much more than a peck.

It felt great, I thought I would feel scared, I know these new feelings have been scary but kissing him didn't, it felt exciting, I have butterflies everytime i see him, even more so when kissing him.

Chapter nine

Gabriel walks into the room, thankfully not when we were kissing, that could have been awkward for everybody. I really want to tell my friends, but while Ollie has a boyfriend I don't want to do that and hurt anybody's feelings.

I don't want Ellis to know i've been kissing his boyfriend, i know i shouldn't have done it a all, and it was wrong, especially since Ellis is my friend, or was my friend but i can't resist Ollie, i don't know what it is about him, he is just amazing, in every single way.

'Hi Gabriel' I say feeling slightly worried about how this is going to go, with Ollie and Gabriel in the same room.
'Hi Noah, Hi Ollie' he replies with a smile

I think that's the first time I've heard Gabriel say hi to Ollie without it being to say something mean, the whole time we were all at mine he didn't say much at all, but at least he was being friendly which was new for Gabriel.

He left way before Ollie did, and as we were cuddling on the bed i look down at Ollie who had his head laying on my chest and his arm wrapped around my waist,

'Ollie, what are we doing, we can't do this, what about Ellis?'

He smiles, moving his hand to touch my cheek

'I broke with with Ellis last week Noah'

At that moment, my heart skipped a beat. Why didn't he just tell me? This changes everything! I always thought I would end up finding a girlfriend, and the reason I hadn't been interested in any of the girls Gabriel tried to set me up with is because I wasn't ready, but now I understand it's because i dont like girls, I like boys, at least I like Ollie.
Ollie turns on to his side so he's facing me, and puts his forehead against mine

'So... Noah'
'Yeah? What's wrong?' i reply, pulling him in a little closer
'I want to ask you something'
'What is it?' i say, leaning back slightly to look at him
'W... will you be my boyfriend?'

I move away and look at him, feeling shocked, but not only shocked but also scared, this makes everything so much more real. Do I want a boyfriend? Is this better being kept as a secret? I know coming out and being in a relationship with a guy is going to be hard, and people are going to judge but I know I shouldn't worry about other people as long as i'm happy, but its not always that simple.

Holding on to Ollie's hands, I lean forward putting my mouth to his ear

Yea, i would like that' i whisper

So, i have boyfriend, something i thought i would never say and now i want to tell people, i really do but i still don't know if i'm actually gay or bisexual all i know is that i've never been interested in girls, well not yet anyway, i have never even been interested in boys, not until i met Ollie.
Going downstairs to where my mum and dad are sitting watching tv, I slowly walk in and sit on the arm of the sofa, looking back and forth between mum and dad trying to build the courage for what i'm about to say.

'Mum..Dad, can I speak to you?'
'Of course Noah, what's wrong?' mum says, looking concerned
'Me and Ollie... were together'
'Together? Like a couple?' Dad asks
Yes dad, a couple' i reply, smiling slightly

Dad gets up and leaves the room. I knew mum would be cooler than dad about this, and I kind of knew this would be his reaction.

'Sorry about your dad sweetheart' mum says, pulling me into a big hug
'Its ok mum, i knew he wouldn't like it but i really like Ollie, and i want to be with him'

Mum has always been really understanding she listens and cares about what i have to say, and cares about my feelings, dad has always wanted me to just follow what everybody else does, what stick with the guys i've been friends with for years, get a girlfriend, and play sports, he tells me he wants me to just be a normal boy, like my friends he definitely doesn't want me to be in a gay relationship.

A few weeks later and me and Ollie are better than ever, spending almost every weekend together as well as after school, it's harder during the day when we are both at school because nobody knows we are together, they don't even know that i'm interested in guys like that, i want to shout it from the rooftops, but i know it wouldn't go down well so we have decided to keep it secret while in school at least, it is really really hard going a full day without hugging, kissing or holding Ollies hand, but we make it work.

Now me and Ollie have been together for just over a month and i fall more and more in love with him everyday, i know i said it.. Love, it's only been a month but I'm pretty sure this is just that. But I would never say I love you first. Imagine if he thought it was too soon, I could not handle the shame.
At school the following Monday everything goes the same as it normally would, i meet Ollie, we walk to school together, go to lessons together, everyone thinking we are just best friends.

Chapter ten

I still meet up with Gabriel and Max but only because i want to keep things as normal as possible, at school at least.
Sometimes I think Ollie finds it hard, he is openly gay, and the whole school knows it. They know he was dating Ellis, of course he says it's ok but i think it hurts him deep down that he can't be open with me. I'm just not ready to share something that big yet.

Gabriels mum and dad planned a weekend away for his birthday, and he could choose a few friends to go along too. Of course he chose me and Max. I wasn't sure about going at first, but mum said it would do me good. I didn't even know where this weekend trip was taking place, and I wouldn't be able to speak to Ollie properly all weekend, which hasn't happened in the last six months, and will I even be able to handle spending a whole weekend with Gabriel and Max.

Arriving at Gabriel's birthday location, I quickly realise we are in the middle of what looks like a forest staying in a small cabin-like house, i get my phone out of my pocket and send Ollie a quick message to let him know we have arrived safely, before deleting all the messages.

I know sometime this weekend Gabriel will end up going through my phone, because he always does! And if he knew about me and Ollie it would ruin his birthday. Not only that, I have to stay here with him for a whole forty-eight hours and that would just be awful for everybody.

Once Gabriels mum and dad leave, he picks up his backpack and opens the zip slightly showing us the three bottles of vodka he has hidden in there. I look towards Max, and then back to Gabriel.

'Does your mum know you brought alcohol?'
'No, of course she doesn't,' Gabriel replies, laughing.

Max looks at me, nudging my arm with his

'We have more people coming later too'
'More people? Like who?
'Don't worry Noah, just have fun for once'

Just have fun for once? I do have fun, but my idea of fun isn't getting drunk, i have never been drunk, but i have seen Gabriel when he has been, and it was nothing but embarrassing. People soon started to arrive, and by the time an hour had passed, there were more than thirty people in this small cabin. While everybody is sitting, talking and drinking, I get my phone out and realise I have five new messages from Ollie, opening them i read them one by one.

08:55pm   'i hope your having a good time, i miss you'
08:59pm   'I know you can't reply while you're with 'the boys' but it's boring without you here'
09:12pm   'I'm wearing your hoodie, it smells like you xx'
09:16pm   'i'm going to sleep now, i'll speak tomorrow xx'
09:20pm   'Noah, just do you know.. I love you, like a lot.. Just so you know xx'

Starting at my phone in disbelief for a few minutes because Ollie hasd just told me he loves it, Gabriel walks in and tried to grab my phone from my hand

'Come and enjoy the party! Put your phone away!'

Putting my phone back into my pocket, I walk over to where most of the other people are standing, when Gabriel hands me a shot.

'No thanks' i say shaking my head
'Go on! Don't be a wimp!'

Taking the shots from Gabriel's hand and quickly drinking it, it tasted awful, burning my throat as it went down. Gabriel is quick to hand me another, clearly trying to get me drunk. I guess I am not good at peer pressure, particularly when I have a group of around ten people staring at me, because I know it i have done eight shots of vodka. I now know what being drunk feels like, I felt hot, slightly dizzy and strangely happy.
When I heard Gabriel calling me, I walked as best I could through to where everybody was sitting in a big circle on the floor.

'Come sit down Noah, truth or dare' Gabriel said with a huge grin spread across his face

Sitting down in the circle, not quite sure whats going , i was starting to feel very nauseous,

'Truth or dare Noah?' Gabriel said, looking at me
'Oh i'm not playing, i'll just watch'
'Come on, are you scared? Truth or dare?'
'Ok, fine, dare' I probably should have said the truth, but Gabriel would have asked a question about Ollie. I figured it would be better to do a stupid dare.
'I dare you to kiss Narla' I could hear some of the girls giggling.

Looking up from my lap. I can't kiss Narla, I have a boyfriend!

'Come on quickly Noah' Gabriel shouts.

Before I can say anything else Narla is in front of me, leaning in to kiss me, so I just kissed her because what else can I do? Say oh sorry.. I can't kiss you. I'm with Ollie.

Chapter eleven

I feel instant regret, standing up to leave, why did I do that? Now it's going to be all around the school when we go back next week, why am I so stupid!
Walking away from the circle, not making eye contact with anybody.

'I'm going to bed, i don't feel good'
'Do you want Narla to join you?' Gabriel says, everybody laughing along.

Walking into the bedroom and slumping myself down on bed I pull my phone out from my pocket. Ollie hasn't sent any more messages since the last, clicking back on the last message sent, the only one I hadn't deleted and reading over it again.

"Noah, just so you know, i love you, like a lot, just so you know xxx"

I start to type out a reply.

'I love you too' I hover my finger over the send button for a few minutes before pressing send, quickly putting my phone face down on the bedside table.
I love Ollie, oh my god, I really love him, I shouldn't be here kissing my ex-girlfriend, I should be at home with my boyfriend, my boyfriend who I love.
I probably should have just told Ollie, it was just a dare after all, it's not like it wasnt to kiss her.
Waking up the next morning, my head pounding, my stomach feeling like it did when i had food poisoning in spain, i roll over so im laying on my stomach getting my phone out from bedside table, no replies from Ollie, its ten am and he hasn't replied, he is always awake early, he would have seen my reply before now.
Twenty instagram notifications? I hardly use Instagram, at least not to post anything. Did I do it last night in my drunk state? Clicking on the app, I can see I had been tagged in a picture, and that was what had gotten all the likes and comments, a picture Gabriel had tagged me in, something from the party no doubt. Gabriel likes to show off, but why where there so many comments, his normal posts only get a couple of likes and comments, clicking on the notification i feel a little more sick than i did before, a picture of me and Narla kissing, a pictures i didn't even know had been taken, Gabriel captioned the picture 'love birds' quickly clicking on to Ollies name in my contact list and pressing call, no answer, he must have seen the picture, of course he has been the picture!
Jumping up from the bed and walking down to Gabriel's bedroom, i slam the door open

'What the hell have you done!' i shout across the room

Sitting up in bed and rubbing his eyes to focus on me,

'What do you mean? It was just a laugh, you know that'
'Just a laugh! Everybody has seen it!'

Just as I turn to leave the room I hear another voice, turning back slowly to look at Narla, they are both laying on the bed, quilt up under their armpits, naked shoulders and a pile of clothes on the floor.

'Gabriel is sorry Noah, he will delete the video' she says, quietly
'It's too late!'

Walking out of the room and back to my own, calling mum on the way there, not wanting to stay there for another night, everytime i'm with Gabriel, something always happens.

'Hi mum, can you come and get me please?' i ask desperately
'Why? What's up darling?' mum asks, concerned tone to her voice
'I'll explain later, can you please just come and pick me up'
'Ok, i'll be there in an hour'

Packing everything into my bag and sitting by the front door waiting for my mum to arrive, Gabriel walks over from the bedroom, still half naked with just a towel wrapped around his waist.

'Where are you going?'
'My Mum's now coming to get me, I can't stay here'
'Because of a stupid video? Why does it even matter? I don't know why your so upset over it'
'Maybe because I didn't want that picture out there, for everybody to see!'
'Do you have a girlfriend, is that why?'
'No Gabriel, I don't have a girlfriend!' technically i'm not lying.
'So what is it then? Why does it matter that I posted the video?'

By now Narla and Max are also standing close by listening to the conversation, I stand up and walk towards Gabriel, dropping my bag onto the floor in front of me.

'You really want to know why?'

Gabriel just nods his head, as if to say 'yes'

'I don't have a girlfriend, i have a boyfriend'

Gabriel looks over to Max and Narla, who are looking just as shocked if not more than Gabriel, he looks like he might cry. I just stand in front of them waiting for somebody to say something, Gabriel makes a sound like he's clearing his throat.

'Ollie?' he asks in a quiet voice

'Yeah Ollie, Ollies my boyfriend, and he's seen your stupid video!'
'I have deleted it now'
'It's too late Gabriel, he's seen it, he's ignoring me!'

Hearing my mum beep the horn of the car outside, I pick up my bag and walk outside to the car.

'Hi mum, thanks for coming to get me'
'Thats ok darling, what's happened?' mum asks, putting her hand on my shoulder
'Gabriel posted a video and now Ollie is ignoring me'
I can't tell mum I was drunk, but I also can't say I kissed Narla while being sober.

'Gabriel brought alcohol yesterday, and invited loads of people from school, everybody got a little bit drunk'

Mum looks at me with a concerned look on her face

'You got drunk?'
'I drank a little, but Gabriel decided to play truth or dare, and i was dared to kiss Narla'
'And you did?' she asks, frowning at me
Yes, and Gabriel filmed it and posted it on Instagram'
'And Ollie has seen the video?' she adds
'Yes, he must have he's ignoring me, i've sent him loads of messages and tied to call him, i think i've really messed this up mum'

By now I have tears running down my face.

'I can't lose him mum'

Mum grabs me into her arms and holds me tight,

'It will be ok darling, you need to speak to him'
'Can you drop me at Ollie's please?' i say, barely able to get my words out through sobbing

Mum nods, giving me a quick kiss on the forehead, I don't know what I'm supposed to say or do to make this right, I have really messed up, I know I need Ollie, my life is nothing without him in it.
I knock on Ollie's front door, but nobody answers. He must know it's me, his mum and dad are never really home, his mum is always working, and his dad works away and isnt home very often. Opening the letter box I shout through hoping he will hear me.

'Ollie, please speak to me'

I'm sitting on the doorstep with my head in my hands when the door slowly opens, turning and looking up at Ollie standing there. It's clear he's been crying, his eyes are bloodshot and his face puffy and red.
I quickly stand up and walk towards him,

'Can i come in please?'

He nods and walks away from the front door, walking into the kitchen and sitting on a counter stool.

'I'm so sorry Ollie, I no what i did is really bad, and i understand if you don't want to be with anymore, but i had to speak to you first'

Looking down at his lap, tears running down his cheeks, I took my hand from my pocket, putting it on his knee.

'Ollie I'm really really sorry'
'Why did you kiss her? Do you still like her?' he says through sobs
'No, of course I don't like her! You know what Gabriel is like, i got drunk and he made us play truth or dare'

He looks up at me, scratching his head

'You got drunk?'
'Yes, and i wish i had never gone i didn't want to kiss Narla, i don't like her Ollie, i love you'

I never thought those words would come from my mouth, but it feels amazing to tell him exactly how I feel. He puts his hand on top of mine, still on his knee and squeezes tightly.

'You really love me?' he asks, clearly not believing me.
'Yes Ollie, i really love you' i say, now laughing

Taking his face in my hands, I kissed him then stood looking into his eyes for a few seconds.

'I have missed you so much, I'm never going away without you again!'

Ollie is smiling now, his face still red and puffy from crying, but he is smiling, Holding him in my arms for what feels like half an hour. I just love him so much.

'Oh, and guess what?' i say excitedly
'What? It's nothing else bad is it?' he replies, a small smile on his face
'No, I told Gabriel I had a boyfriend, I told him you were my boyfriend, oh and Max and Narla may have heard too' I say, kissing him on the nose.

Standing up from the stool he's sitting on, he throws his arms around my neck,

'You mean we can be together, like properly?' he says with the biggest grin on his face now,
'I mean.. Yes, we were together properly anyway, but we can do that in school now too' i
laugh.
*'Are you sure you want to do this? You were straight before you met me, you don't just feel
sorry for me?'*
*'Ollie don't be silly, i obviously wasn't straight, you are the most amazing person i have met
in my whole life, and i want to be with you'*
'Do you want to stay here tonight?' he ask's putting his arm around my back
'Yes, of course i do, i wasn't planning on heading home anyway'
'Do you want to watch a film and cuddle?' Ollie asks sweetly
'Yes! As long as we can watch something scary!'
'You know i don't like horrors, Noah!'
'It's ok, I'll protect you' I say, pulling him into a hug.

Laying upstairs on the bed, we end up watching a film Ollie likes, he is so scared of horror
films it's actually cute, and of course i end up watching it alone while Ollie sleeps with his
head laying on my chest and his arms wrapped around me.
I pick my phone up and take a selfie, making sure to show Ollie's head in the photo as well as
me and post it to Instagram with the caption 'he's so cute when he sleeps'

Of course the first person to comment is my mum, she's my biggest supporter, the only
people who knew about me and Ollie before was my mum and dad, and then Gabriel, Max
and Narla and now everybody on my Instagram will see it.
Instead of feeling scared like I thought I would, I feel relieved, happy, like a weight has been
lifted.
Waking up the next morning, Ollie has already gotten up like he always does. He wakes
around six and sits on the bed eating toast and drinking tea until I wake up.
Sitting up, I slide my hand under the pillow to grab my phone which is where I left it the
night before, it wasn't there anymore.
Ollie looks towards me, opening his hand with my phone in it.

'I'm sorry' he says, looking down into his lap
'Why are you sorry?'
'I was looking through your phone, you know after everything with Narla i..'

Shuffling over to sit next to him, i put my arm around his back

'It doesn't matter, i love you Ollie, i don't want anybody else i promise'

A lot of people would feel uncomfortable with their partner secretly checking their phone
while they sleep. I guess it's a trust thing, but I have broken Ollie's trust, and I need to make
him believe it's him I want, nobody else.

Chapter twelve

'Ollie, did you see the Instagram post?'
'What post?' he asks looking confused, like something else bad is about to come out
'Check your phone' i say smiling

He unlocks his phone and clicks on the notification, staring at the picture for a few minutes before standing up and jumping on top of me.

'I'll get you back for that' he says laughing
'But you look cute, and i want to show my boyfriend off to the world!'
'We have to go back to school tomorrow, are you going to be ok?'
'Of course I am' I say , grabbing onto his hand.

Ollie has been worried about me coming out to everybody, and asks almost daily if I'm sure I want to do this, which of course I do, but he struggled a lot when he came out himself, a lot of people bullied him, he doesn't want that for me.
The biggest thing for me was telling Gabriel, I knew how he would react, and that only came out because of an argument, if not me and Ollie would still be hiding it from everybody. So the argument did some good, although not in the best way for me, what with the whole Narla situation. Me and Ollie are stronger than ever, he is learning to trust me again, he has no reason not to, because I would never be silly enough to hurt him ever again! It broke my heart seeing him so sad, all because of my silly actions.

The next day at school is a little different, I walk into school holding ollies hand, if i'm being honest i was a little nervous, but Ollie always seems to calm my nerves, like he knows how to say the right things to calm me down instantly, I love that about him, we had a lot of stares, people whispering to their friends as we walked through the school corridors but we just ignored it, we are happy and that's all that matters, to me anyway. And of course, we walk towards Gabriel and Max and a few of their other friends, Ollie tries to move his hand away from mine, thinking it would be best if they didn't see that, but i grab his hand back, even tighter, looking at him and smiling as we walk past, and to my surprise they say nothing at all. The first day back at school in an openly gay relationship wasn't as bad as i thought it would be, we got the odd idiot asking why i had 'suddenly decided' to become gay, or if Ollie has turned me, which we just ignored, but otherwise everyone else was pretty cool, some people who we had never spoken to before, spoke to us, out of this whole situation that I was so worried about, we have also made some new friends too.

A couple of days later, sitting in the kitchen talking to my mum, my phone rings, its Ollie,

'Hi Ollie'

I can barely hear what he's saying though cries,

'What's wrong Ollie? Are you ok?'
'No nothing is ok' he says, his voice is shaky
'Ollie, what's happened?' I'm now pacing the kitchen, mum can see the worry on my face.

All i can hear is him crying down the phone, and to be honest i'm really starting to panic, i hang up the phone and look at my mum.

'Mum, can you drop me off a Ollie's please'
'Is everything ok Noah? He sounded upset'
'I don't know, i need to go and see him'

I get out of my mums car and run up to Ollies front door and just as i'm about to knock, he opens the door, he is in a state and it makes me panic a little more, he was upset when the stuff after Gabriel's party happened, but i've never seen him this upset, walking into the house, he goes up to his bedroom as i follow behind.
'What's wrong Ollie? Have I done something wrong?' He walks over so he's closer to me and puts his head onto my shoulder and his arms wrapped around my back, I lift his head with my hands and wipe his tears away. With my hands still on his face,
'Ollie, please tell me what's wrong, your worrying me'
'I love you Noah, please don't forget that'

What the hell is going on? Why is he talking like this, and why is he crying so much? Something really bad must have happened this time.

'Noah, my mum and dad broke up'
'I'm so sorry' I say, hugging him tighter.
'Mum says we have to move to Scotland'
I move back and look at Ollie,
'Scotland??'
'Yeah, I finally find you, the love of my life and she makes me move away from you'
He's now crying even harder, I'm even starting to cry a little, 'How can I get through every day without you Ollie?'
'I'm so sorry Noah, do you want to end this now, you know, to save anymore hurt'
'NO, I do not want to end this now, if your moving away, I want to spend every single minute of every day with you before you have to leave me'
'Can we still be together, you know when i'm gone, like long distance?'

I lean forward and kiss him on the forehead,

'Yes Ollie, we are not going to break up, nothing can break us up'

His crying had calmed down a little now, I think he was more worried about my reaction but whether he is living ten minutes up the road, or in Scotland i will be with Ollie, no matter what.

Sitting on the end of Ollies bed, holding on to his hand

'So when do you need to leave? How long do we have?'
'We are going next week Noah' he says, starting to look sad again.

NEXT WEEK? I have fallen in love with this boy, like head over heels in love and he has to leave me to move to Scotland in a week! I don't want to upset him any further so I just try and change the subject, but in the back of my head its the only thing I can think about, and it's breaking my heart.

The weekend went by quicker than i think any weekend ever has, and i think that's because i know in just five days i have to say goodbye, we spent the whole weekend laying in bed, watching movies, cuddling, kissing and talking, knowing it would be out last weekend that we would be able to do this.

The day before Ollie is supposed to leave, I wake up feeling sick, anxious and tired after barely sleeping the night before. I hadn't told my mum yet about Ollie leaving, I think she had figured something was wrong, but she hadn't asked any questions.

Walking down the stairs, i shout though to the kitchen,

'Mum, i'm now going to meet Ollie'
'Don't you want breakfast Noah?'
'I need to go, I don't have time' I say while opening the front door.
'What's going on Noah? Is everything ok with you and Ollie?'

I don't want to speak about it again, because I cry every time I even think about him leaving tomorrow.

'Ollie is moving away mum'
'Moving away? Where is he moving?'
'He's moving to Scotland tomorrow'

Mum just looks at me, shocked expression on her face, she puts her hand on my shoulder,

'Are you ok darling?'
'Not really mum, my boyfriend is moving away, and i'll probably never see him again, i'm definitely not ok'

As i was towards Ollies house, i can see his mum loading suitcases in to the car, this is all starting to feel very real now, i walk towards her and smile,

'Hi Sandra'
'Oh hi Noah, are you ok?'

Am I ok? Of course I'm not ok, nothing about this is ok!

'Is Ollie inside?' I ask
'Yeah, hes upstairs finishing his packing, go straight up'

I walk up the stairs and into Ollie's bedroom, he is sitting on the edge of his bed sorting through his jumpers, his room full of boxes and duffel bags with all his clothes packed inside.

'Hi, are you almost ready to leave now?' I say, putting my head round the corner of the door.
'I really don't want to go Noah, i want to stay with you'

We both laugh, turning to sit on the floor, leaning against the bed Ollie sits next to me, putting his head on my shoulder,

'I really love you Noah, I don't want you to ever forget that' ollie says, moving his hand to my knee.
'I love you too, and how could I ever forget you!'

I take out my phone from my pocket and turn the camera to face us, putting my arm around Ollie's neck and pulling him closer to me, i snap a photo, then set it as my home screen.

'There, now i'll never forget you'
'Can we text, and facetime, like everyday?'
'Of course we can Ollie, and promise me you wont meet anyone better than me!'
'There is no one in this world better than you' he says, kissing me on the cheek

The next morning, Ollie is leaving early so i make sure i'm up early and at his house before he leaves, just as i arrive Ollie's mum is loading all the last bags in to the car, Ollie sitting on the doorstep watching as his mum struggle to squeeze everything into the car boot.
Walking up to the door, I sit next to Ollie, now realising this is it, he is leaving today.

'You know, i'm going to miss you, like a lot!' i say, holding on to Ollies hand
'I'm going to miss you more' he laughs

I had just got here when his mum shouts up the path towards him using hand gestures to tell him to hurry up,

'Ollie, time to go!'

I stand up, Ollie standing behind me, he grabs on to me, harder than he ever has before and hugs me for a whole ten minutes while his mum is demanding he leaves. I put my head into his neck and whisper into his ear.

'I love you, so so much'

He moves his head back, and kisses me the last kiss we will probably ever have,

'I love you too, and I always will,' he says with his forehead against mine.

Then walking away, he gets into his mum's car and before I know it he's gone, on his way to Scotland and I'm here, alone.

I slowly walk to school, checking my phone every few minutes for any messages from Ollie, i have never felt heartbreak before, but I'm pretty sure this is what it feels like. I haven't even broken up with my boyfriend, we are still very much together just not in person anymore. I don't hear anything from Ollie for the whole day, or even that night but he is travelling and the signal is probably not great so i don't think to much into it, but the next morning i wake up to three missed calls and six messages, i must have fallen asleep and not heard my phone.

12:08am   'We have arrived in Scotland, I want to come home already!'
12:11am   'i love you Noah, and i miss you already'
12:14am   'Please wake up, i want to hear your voice xxx'
12:22am   'NOAH! Wake up!'
12:30am   'i'm going to try sleep now, i wish i was with you xxxx'
12:35am   'i love you'

As soon as i wake up, i quickly reply to his messages

07:11am   'Hi, i've just woken up, i'm glad you arrived safe, i'm sorry i didn't wake up when you texted i feel asleep really early, i think it was because i didn't sleep the night before, i don't know if your awake now, but if you are still sleeping i hope your sleeping well, and i love you xx'

It's three weeks later, three whole weeks without Ollie! We text and facetime all the time but it's not the same. I miss him so much I actually cry sometimes, and if I'm being honest I'm struggling without him here.
I know that makes me sound selfish. I'm happy for him, happy that he gets to live in a new place, go to a new school, and make new friends but I'm jealous at the same time that they get to be with him and I don't.
My mum is noticing that i'm not myself at the minute, she asks constantly if im ok, teachers at school have also shown their concern, im skipping lessons, and sometimes i don't even go to school at all.

Chapter thirteen

Ollie is trying to be supportive all the way from Scotland, mum told him i'm struggling which i wish she hadn't, i no to some people it may seem stupid, but without Ollie i am miserable, and i don't know how to change that.

08:00am   'Noah, are you up and ready for school? Xx'
08:06am   'yeah, i'm ready, leaving soon xx'
08:22am   'I know you're not, your mum said you're still in bed!'

Ok, so now my mum and Ollie are discussing my depressive state. Dad thinks I'm just being stupid because it was just a 'teenage fling'. If it was just that, then why do I feel like my world is ending? Why does Ollie not feel like this?

09:12am   'i'm on my way to school now, a little late, but im on my way'
09:20am   'if you need me, message me although i am miles away, i'm here for you Noah, whenever you need me xx'
09:30am   'i love you xx'
09:32am   'i love you too xxxx'

I did a whole day without skipping any lessons, which hadn't happened for a whole month since Ollie left. Sitting outside on the bench at break time, Gabriel and Max walked towards me and sat on the opposite side of the bench.

'Alright Noah?' Gabriel says
'Yeah, i'm good'
'Where's Ollie? Haven't seen him in a while'
'He's moved to Scotland'
'So now you're single again, need any help finding a new girlfriend.. Or boyfriend'
'No, i'm not single, i am still with Ollie'

Getting up i walk way, this is exactly why i have been avoiding school because i knew this would come up people would be asking about Ollie, i was feeling ok today, but then Gabriel had to open his big mouth and make everything crap again, because that's what Gabriel always does, make everything crap.

02:56pm   'I did a full day today, and it was awful!'
03:01pm   'What happened? Are you ok?
03:10pm   'Just Gabriel, I'm fine'
03:14pm   'What did he do?'

| 03:22pm | 'he just asked if i was single now, and wanted to play matchmaker like he used too' |
| 03:31pm | 'I hate him so much!' |

Three months passed, three whole months without Ollie, he's in his new school and has made some new friends and I'm really happy for him. I'm doing much better now too. I still have days where I'm sad, and feel angry but that has been much less than before.

Mum was really worried about me at the beginning, and she reminds me of that everyday which doesn't always help.

I was staying in my bedroom, watching my phone for Ollie to call or text, crying a lot, and genuinely just feeling crap about everything.

I have made a couple of new friends at school too, who have helped me massively and Ollie is happy that I'm finally not spending all my time alone. I think deep down he was really worried too.

My dad was still acting like the idiot he has always been, telling me now Ollies gone I can finally focus on finding a nice girl. There were a few times I wanted to scream in his face that I was gay, but that would cause more bad than good. Mum was always there to stick up for me though.

Me and ollie still stay in contact daily, not as much as before because he's a lot more busy now hes back in school and had lots of new cool friends to hang around with, i'm not jealous, honestly, i'm over that now.

SIx months later, and ten months since I had last seen Ollie, how has it almost been a whole year! I still love him as much as I did the day he left, nothing has changed my end but Ollie seems to have gotten more distant. Who can blame him? I knew deep down this would happen eventually, but I didn't want to think about it because I knew how much it would hurt, a whole never level of hurt Ollie, the love of my life is growing out of love with me. I don't want to slump back in to my depression, but i can't help it, that dark feeling is back, the feeling of sadness, like i don't want to carry on without Ollie again, i no it sounds dramatic, it probably is, but Ollie was my first love, and i wanted him to be my last.

I'm spending more and more time in my room again, and everybody around me is noticing I don't care though I need to get over this myself.

Mum walks into my room the next morning to let me know she's booked me a doctor's appointment. Why do I need a doctor's appointment? I'm fine! I only attend because I know it would hurt mum more if I refused.

Arriving at the doctors surgery, me and mum sit in the waiting room waiting for the doctor to call my name,

'Noah Bradshaw'

Standing up from my seat, i turn to mum,

'Are you coming in with me?'

Mum nods, and holds on to my arm walking towards the doctors room with me. I am old enough now that I should be able to attend my own doctor's appointment, but when I'm feeling vulnerable mum always knows what to say.

'Hi Noah, I'm Doctor Jones, how are you today?'
'Im ok' i shrug

Mum looks at me with a confused expression on her face, she knows I'm far from ok!

'He's been suffering with what I think is depression' mum blurts out before I have a chance to say anything else, I look toward mum and then back to Dr Jones who is now staring right at me.

'Is that how you feel Noah?' she asks
'I guess, I mean... My boyfriend left to move to Scotland.. And everything has been bad since he left'

I can feel tears welling in my eyes, every time i think or speak about Ollie, this happens so i just tend to not think about any of it and keep it in the back of my mind.

'That can be hard Noah, but you shouldn't make yourself unwell over it' Dr Jones says while looking at her computer screen, tapping her pen on the desk.

'He's been locking himself in his room for days on end, not going to school, and when he does he skips all of his lessons, I've been really worried about him' mum says to the doctor, sounding like she might cry herself.

I don't know why she has to tell the doctor all of this, she's making me look like a lovesick teenager and I am not that!

'Would you be happy if I prescribed you some medication Noah? Something to help a little with the feelings your having'

'Medication?' I look towards mum and whisper to her.

The room falls silent for a few seconds before mum looks up at the doctor and smiles

'He can give it a try'
'It can make him feel a little bit sleepy to begin with, sometimes a little disoriented, but those side effects will pass quickly' the doctor says, look back and forth between me and mum.

Back in the car on the way home i look at mum angrily,

'I'm not taking medication, I don't need it!'

'Please Noah, just try it, it doesn't work you can stop but please just try'

After everything mum has done for me, stuck up for me when dad has been a homophobic idiot, helped me when I was at my lowest when Ollie first left, I guess I can try, what harm can it do.

I took the first tablet that evening, mum was watching over me like a hawk to make sure I actually swallowed it. Before now I had been scared to even take a painkiller and now here I am taking antidepressants. At first I felt fine, well.. No different than before, but after an hour or so I start to feel anxious, shaky and agitated, a feeling that makes me want to never take those tablets again.

Mum tells me it's the side effects and they will wear off after a week or so, but i do not want to deal with this for a week! I would rather feel depressed.

The next morning the effects of last nights medication had slightly worn off, still feeling anxious, a feeling in the pit of my stomach that i can't put my finger on,it's been two whole days since Ollie last messaged or called me, which is not like him at all, it's only eight am and i have already sent four messages to him with no reply, although i can see he's opened them.

07:12am   'Good morning, did you sleep ok? Xxx'
07:14am   'I got some new medication from the doctors yesterday, its making me feel really strange'
07:20am   'Are you ok? I haven't heard from you in two days!!'
07:45am   'Please call me, i need to speak to you xxxx'

Ive never gone longer than four hours without speaking to Ollie, now he is completely ignoring me, has he had enough of me? Maybe I should just give him some space and he will message me in his own time? Making my way downstairs for breakfast, mum is standing by the kitchen door, pills in hand ready to stick one in my mouth, almost like she heard me get off the bed and had to be there, ready.

'Good morning Noah, how do you feel?'
'I'm fine' i say, abruptly
I have your medication ready'
'I can see that!'

Of course I take medication to keep mum happy, but now I have to go to school while feeling like i'm on another planet.

I somehow got through the whole day, i'm not sure how though, I actually nodded off sitting in maths a couple of times.

Chapter fourteen

It's been another whole day, and with no contact from Ollie at all, walking through the front door and into the kitchen, I slump myself down on a bar stool.

'Mum, has Ollie called the house phone?'

Dad looks over to me, looking almost annoyed that i had even mentioned Ollies name,

'Just forget about Ollie, Noah, he's gone!'

Mum gives dad a stare, a stare as if to say 'shut up!'
He doesn't understand he never had really understood me. When I was in year eight and i didnt want to join the school football team, he almost forced me too, and I absolutely hated every minute of it, until I just quit and didn't tell him for almost a year.
And now his only son is gay, and he hates the thought of that. He has always wanted me to get a nice girlfriend, so when he found out that me and Narla were together he was ecstatic! But now I'm with Ollie, it's like he almost hates me, but I've got used to that.

It's another two days later, and Ollie has still not sent a single message. I've also stopped sending him messages because I don't want to annoy him, he clearly doesn't want to talk to me.
Laying in bed that evening, watching youtube on tv with my phone laying on my chest, the doorbell rings, jumping up off the bed and to the bannister i look over as dad answers the door, thinking he has just ordered a take away, or had an amazon delivery, which he has almost daily.

'Mr Bradshaw, is Ollie home?'

I no that voice from anywhere, i run down the stairs as quickly as i can, almost falling when i reach the bottom shoving dad out of the way on my way past,

'Ollie!'
'Hi Noah' he says, massive gin spread across his face
I thought you didn't want to speak to me anymore'

Dad is still standing behind me, listening to the whole conversation

'Come in, let's go upstairs' i say to Ollie, putting my hand out to grab him
'I have missed you so much Noah'
'I thought you wanted to break up with me' i say, looking down at our hands touching

'Why would I want to break up with you?'
'I...I just thought that because you hadn't spoken to me for days..'
'I've been travelling home, I wanted to surprise you, and I knew if I messaged I wouldn't be able to keep it a surprise!' he says, leaning in and kissing my forehead
'How long are you here for?'
'We are staying! Mum decided Scotland wasn't for her, and i needed to be back here with you'

Now I have the biggest grin on my face, i put my hand on Ollie's face and kiss him like I've never kissed him before.

'I love you so much, please never leave again'
'I promise' he says, linking his pinky finger to mine.

Sleeping with Ollie in my arms that night, something I haven't done for almost a year, and the feelings were still as strong as they were the day he left. I thought this would break us, but it just made us stronger and my love for him is so much more intense.
Being away from Ollie for as long as I did, made me realise he is in fact the love of my life and I wasn't just going crazy like my family believed.
Ollie also said he felt sad and angry, just like I did, my emotions went a little bit of a rollercoaster, maybe it was just the fact Ollie had gone, maybe it was other things added in.
I had to deal with my dad telling me I wasn't gay almost daily, and when I tried to explain he would just brush it off and walk away.
Maybe I needed my dad just to let me be me, without hating me, maybe I just needed to ignore everything he said and be happy without his blessing.

If I had not met Ollie, I would probably still be going through the same cycle of Gabriel finding the next girlfriend for me, hanging around on the field and spending the school holidays sitting at home doing nothing at all.

Ollie changed all of that, i now have a boyfriend who i love so much, and Gabriel has finally come to terms that i am gay, and i am happy he even speaks to Ollie occasionally, and the last half term me and Ollie spent the whole time together, between both of our houses.
He really is amazing, and I can't thank him enough for being the love of my life, not only that but making me love myself too.

Chapter sixteen

A year later

Me and Ollie have been together for two years now, and we are still very much in love. A lot of people doubted us and thought we wouldn't last, but we have proven them wrong.
We are both eighteen in our second year of sixth form before we both head off to university.
We have a great friend group, my mum absolutely loves Ollie, and has made him feel like one of our family, while my dad still thinks i'm having a 'gay phase' i thought he would be past all that now, it has been two years!
We have had hundreds of dates, two holidays together, one with my family, and one with Ollies, who are also lovely. Lots of kissing, and of course lots of being intimate with each other, which is my favourite part of everyday, but don't tell Ollie that, he doesn't like me talking about anything that involves too much affection, it's so sweet how embarrassed he gets.
I remember once, when we were in Turkey on holiday with Ollie's parents, everybody sitting around the table waiting for dinner to arrive when Ollie's dad started the discussion on safe sex, Ollie looked like he wanted the ground to swallow him up there and then.
Of course I know, it's a good subject to learn about what we did in school, but maybe not so much from your dad, and especially not on a family holiday, but Ollie's dad, he found it funny that Ollie was mortified.
I wish my dad was more like Ollie's dad, he is so lucky to have that and sometimes i find myself lost in a daydream wishing my dad was just like him.
I have Ollie's dad, if i need to speak to anybody about anything, he is always there for me, and has helped in some situations that my own dad wouldn't and i can't thank him enough for that, he is simply great.
I think the message should be out there now, that I'm in love with a boy I thought would never even be interested in me, but I'm so lucky he gave me that chance to love him, and I do more than anything in the world.
I can't wait for Ollie's side of the story to be told, and I hope he loves me just as much as I love him.

Printed in Great Britain
by Amazon

18582107R00037